Fly
Like the Wind

Written and Illustrated
by
Bridgette Z. Savage

PUBLISHED BY
BUCKBEECH STUDIOS
STANFORD, INDIANA

For information, contact the publisher:
Buckbeech Studios
P.O. Box 430
Stanford, IN 47463
www.buckbeech.com

Printed by World Arts, Inc.
Spencer, Indiana

Cover and book design by Charles J. Savage

Library of Congress control number: 2005905901

ISBN 0-9771494-0-4

Second Printing

Available online and in bookstores.
For quantity orders and discounts contact the publisher.

Dedicated to
all the brave horses of the Civil War,
who gave so much without understanding why.

Bridgette Z. Savage

Fly
Like the Wind

Prologue

In Southern Indiana, down near where the Ohio River meets the Wabash River, there is an old, old town. It is called New Harmony. I'm sure that I could write a lot of stories about all that happened there, but this one story that I need to tell you is about a man and his life-long friend. It's a story about how friendship can go on and on, beyond the lifetimes of the friends.

In New Harmony, there is a building called the Working Men's Institute. It is made of brick, and has a tall square tower. There is an arch made of limestone over the giant front doors. Nine limestone steps lead up from the sidewalk to the entryway. Sometimes a cat named Lil is rubbing herself against the front steps, waiting for people to come and say "What an unusual looking cat!" That's what she was doing one day when I walked up the sidewalk, under the shade trees, and went up the steps to the front door.

Even though the door was twice as tall as I am, when I put my thumb on the latch and pushed gently, it swung open without a sound, as if it didn't weigh a thing. I was in a sunny entry room, at the bottom of a stairway, and on my right I could see a library, with chairs, shelves, books, and oil paintings high on the walls. On my left, there was a set of doors that led to what looked like the offices. The windows were taller than most rooms are nowadays. If you had never heard the word "grand" used to describe a place before, you would know right away that it should be used to describe this one!

The banister of the stairway is smooth, where many hands have slid along the wood. It leads to a museum upstairs. There are different displays in the rooms of this second floor. Some are new, with videotapes about the Wabash River, which has always been so important to this town. Some are old displays, with tags typed neatly on a typewriter. I love museums and collections. One room has lots of antique glass display cases with various collections in them. The cases are all around the walls of the room, and around the center, as well. In the cases, there are fossils, minerals, hundreds of clam shells, a taxidermied red wolf, button-up shoes, a static electricity machine, and all sorts of other things. I noticed some papers on top of one of the cases, and picked them up. One was a picture of a pleasant-looking man in a suit, and the other two pages with typing on both sides were titled "The Story of Old Fly".

I don't know if time has ever stood still for you. It did for me. Time simply did not exist while I read that story. When I got to the end, I looked up, and to my wonder, I realized that the skeleton of the horse, which was directly in front of me, was the one in the story. It was Fly. Her head was tilted slightly. The curiosity and spirit that she had possessed in life were still showing in the posture of those delicate bones posed in the silent room.

This is the story that I must tell you. It is the story of Fly.

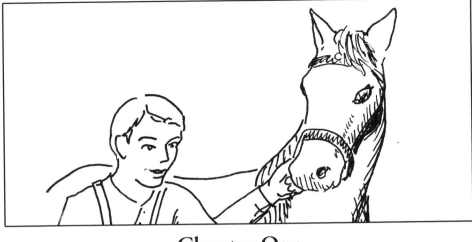

Chapter One
A New Horse

Back in 1855, when this story begins, cars and tractors had not been invented. There were trains pulled by steam locomotives and river boats to move people and freight long distances. Some places had canals, and those had their own sort of boats.

Almost all of the farming was done with horses in those days. The plowing and planting, the harvesting and the hauling: All that work had to be done with real, live, horse power. Mules and oxen were put to work, as well. Some of the draft horses were gigantic, and a full grown man was only as tall as their shoulder. Those horses were for the heaviest work that took the most strength. Other types of horses were called driving horses. They were lightweight and fast, to pull buggies. Many could trot or pace, and looked fancy streaking down the roads with their tails and heads held high, and their glossy manes and tails flowing in the wind. The huge plantations of the South needed riding horses that could travel all day, with a fast, smooth walk that was easy on the rider. There were lots of horses that were in between:

Good-sized, sturdy horses, able to do light draft work, pull a buggy, or be used for a saddle horse.

That was the sort of horse that Mr. G. A. Barrett was looking for when he went to visit the County Farm one warm spring day. He had heard that a mare owned by a lady named Hazel Nelson was for sale, and he wanted to go have a look.

Mr. Barrett was a farmer in Posey County, Indiana. Posey County is rolling farmland, with soft soil that will grow about anything. Corn, wheat, beans, melons, squash and all sorts of food grow well in the tan-colored soil. The Wabash River wiggles down the west side of Posey County, and the Ohio River is on the South side. They meet at the very southwestern tip of Indiana, with Kentucky and Illinois just across the water. Farm produce could be put on a boat and taken on the rivers all the way to Cairo, Illinois, St. Louis, Missouri, Memphis, Tennessee, or even to New Orleans, Louisiana. But it all took work, and that took horses.

Mr. Barrett checked the mare over. Teeth will tell the age of a horse, so you have to check those. If they can't eat, they get weak, so even a young horse has to have good teeth. Feet are important, too. Good hooves are not split and show no signs of disease.

After running his hand over the mare, and putting her through her paces, he put his ear against her side and listened. You have to check their wind, or how they breathe. A horse with bad lungs or heart problems won't be able to keep up with the work that needs done. You have to look at how big their rib cage is to see if they've got enough lung-room. She seemed sound of wind and limb.

It was good that she was also friendly. A horse that doesn't have the heart to work, or doesn't like people is not a good deal. Mrs. Nelson's mare was a fine horse. She was well worth the price. In fact, Mr. Barrett smiled when he thought about the "little extra" that this mare had to offer. He was sure his family would be happy to see him come up the road to the farm that afternoon.

When Mr. Barrett came home from his horse buying trip, the family came out to greet him, and to see the new addition to their farm.

George A. Barrett was married to Minerva and they had eleven children. All of them were amazed to see that the new mare had a baby following her, playing peep-eye with them from behind her mother. Young George M. Barrett was only fourteen when he first saw the little foal following her mother into the barn lot. He knew he liked the little foal right away. She was one week old, dark, with a white star on her forehead, and she was very curious. George was growing up, and ready to do a man's work on the farm.   It was April 11th, and they had already been working hard to get the fields ready for planting.   Mr. Barrett could see that his son was old enough to take the responsibility of owning his own horse, and told him that, as long as the boy would take care of her, the little filly would be his.

Horses are born with long legs, so that they can keep up with the big horses. Back when horses were wild, like zebras, they had to be able to stay with their mothers and travel with the herd. Although horses have been tamed for thousands of years now, they still stand up just as soon as they can when they are born. There are no wild animals chasing herds of horses, like lions do to zebras, but baby horses know that they need to stay close to their mothers, and do what their mothers do, just like baby zebras.

The best way to tell how a horse is going to act is to watch its mother. She is the one who has taught the young horse the most important things it knows.   Mrs. Nelson's

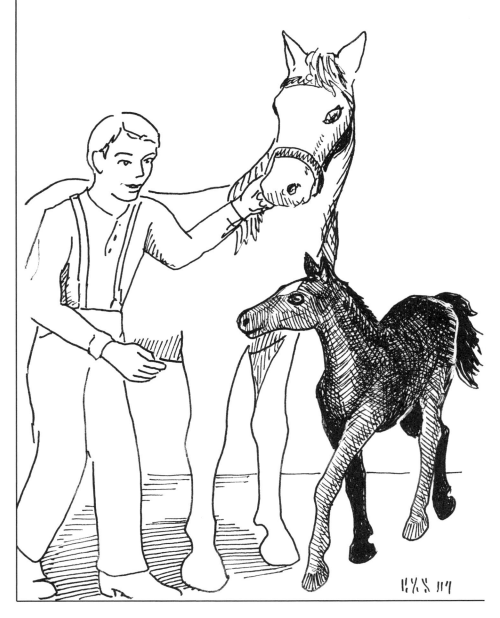

mare liked people, and trusted the people who took care of her. That's how the little foal learned to act the way she would for the rest of her life.

It wasn't long before the young horse had a name. George called her "Fly". When she ran across the pasture, tossing her head, feeling the spring winds as they rippled the grass, George knew that she would be able to "Fly like the Wind" when she grew up. And he knew that he would be with her.

There are lots of things that a horse has to learn and to get used to in order to work well with people. Being groomed, getting brushed and curried, having hooves picked and shoes put on is unnatural to a horse at first. Horses don't like to have their feet handled, because getting a foot stuck in something is the worst thing that can happen to them. Running away is the main way that horses can defend themselves. If they are cornered by an attacker, they can kick and strike out with their hooves, and even bite, but their very first instinct is to run.

Fly got used to the light harness, so that she could pull the buggy in the summer, and the sleigh in the winter. She learned to wear the horse collar, which was like a big, padded oval that went on over her head, and rested on her shoulders. The rest of the harness hooked to the wooden and metal pieces on both sides of the collar, and when she pulled forward, the weight of the load was being pushed by her shoulders. The work harness was heavier than the light harness, but they both were made of leather straps that had to be thrown up on Fly's back, then arranged, and buckled and hooked up the right way.

The most fun was the saddle. When George put the saddle blanket on her back, she knew that they were going somewhere together, not out to the field to work. Sometimes they would go to visit a neighbor, and other times they would go to town, in Stewartsville, New Palestine, or even New Harmony. There were other horses and people in the towns, and when George went into one of the buildings, Fly was tied to a hitching post or tree. She could watch the people, wagons, and other horses go past.

George used to brush her back, and dream of where they would go together.

Even his wildest dreams, however, could not compare with what the two of them would see and do in real life.

Chapter Two
Indiana

Indiana had become a state in 1816, but many people settled in the territory before then. Different groups of Native Americans were already living in Indiana. The Delaware, Shawnee, Piankeshaw, and Potowatomi are some of the native people of Indiana. After all, the name "Indiana" means "Land of the Indians". The rivers were full of fish, some giant ones like the sturgeon and the paddle-fish, and plenty of catfish and bluegill. Along the river banks, otters played and burrowed, and beavers built dams that created lakes on the creeks. Buffalo traveled their ancient path across the bottom part of the state each year, migrating to find fresh pasture.

When settlers started coming in, there were early families, like Tom Lincoln's, who came from Kentucky, and had a very hard time. Land had to be cleared to plant crops, and milk cows grazed in the woods. During these early years, many settlers died from disease or starvation. Sometimes cows would eat poisonous plants, and whole families would get sick or die. That is what had happened to some of Tom

Lincoln's family. Tom was a skilled furniture-maker. Many things like desks, cupboards, and beds that he made can still be seen today. Despite all of his hard work, he ended up taking his son, Abe, and the rest of his family to Illinois. But there were many families that held on in Indiana, built solid log homes, and managed to clear enough land to make crops to feed themselves, and also to sell. George's family was one of the fortunate ones. Their hard work had paid off. What had been wilderness just fifty years before was turning into farms and crossroads towns. In 1825, the State Capitol had changed from Corydon, in the south end of the state, to Indianapolis, which was more in the middle of the state.

Abe Lincoln had gone into politics in Illinois, and had become the President of the United States.

All through the spring of 1861 there was a lot of visiting going on. Some nights Fly could hear the men's voices on the porch of the house after chores. It seemed that they had a lot to talk about. The voices sounded worried, or angry.

Whenever Fly and George went to town, it seemed that people spent their time looking at large pieces of paper with small black marks all over them. People would gather around in little groups and talk to each other. Fly had no idea what they were doing, but she liked the rustling sound of the paper. The noise reminded her of corn shucks. There were also papers tacked to the posts of some buildings, and people would stand and stare at the posts. To Fly, the people reading the posters sort of looked like old horses that dozed off where they had been tied up.

Fly was six years old in 1861. A six year old horse is full grown, and in the prime of life. She had filled out to be a beautiful mare. Her white star shone on her forehead, and her dark mane and tail were thick and healthy. She had neat black hooves, well cared for, and a beautiful straight back.

At the shoulder, she was about 16 hands high. A "hand" is how people measure horses. Each hand is four inches, so Fly was around five feet, four inches tall at the shoulder. She was the color of a fresh apple seed in the sun, and her mane and tail were black. She had grown up to be very fast and smart, just like George had thought she would. George had grown, too. He was twenty that year. He was lean and tall, and he was a fine horseman with a fine horse.

A lot was going on in America during the end of the 1850's. The Northern and Southern states were arguing more and more about how much control the government in Washington, D.C., had over the states. Many compromises had been offered and rejected, until finally, the Southern states declared themselves a separate country and split away from the United States in the spring of 1861. The states that left the Union called themselves the Confederacy, and were led by their own president, Jefferson Davis. Those states that wanted to stay united were called the Union, and were led by the elected president, Abraham Lincoln.

The biggest disagreement was slavery. Would America be a nation that allowed slavery, or a nation of free men? The Southern states had many huge plantations, which grew cotton and tobacco. These giant plantations used many slave laborers to work the land. Smaller family farms of the North raised a wide variety of crops and livestock. When Northern farm families needed help, they hired laborers to work with them. The North also had more factories than the South, so there were other jobs besides farming. Indiana was a free state, which did not allow slavery, but it was just across the Ohio River from the states where slavery was permitted. Because of this, in Indiana there were many houses where slaves who were running away to the North hid. There was a whole route to freedom, from one hiding

place to another, leading through Indiana. This secret route was called "The Underground Railroad", and the people who helped the slaves travel were called "conductors". The conductors would lead the runaways from one "station" to another, always hiding, until they were far enough north to make a new life for themselves.

Slavery had been an issue that people argued about since President George Washington's days, but by the middle of the 1800's, the South depended upon it. With so many new states being added west of the Mississippi, the debate had heated up. When the Confederate States left the Union, the debate had become a war. President Lincoln issued a call for 75,000 troops in April of 1861. In May, he called for 42,000 more.

In June, George and his father had a serious talk. Fly could tell that something was going to happen. Mr. and Mrs. Barrett were quiet, and spoke softly to each other. The women seemed sad, in an odd way.

In July, George and Fly saddled up for a long ride. Fly thought it was strange that there was so much hugging and hand holding involved in leaving the farm that day. Something very different than she had ever seen before must be happening.

On the 21st of July, they were in Evansville, Indiana, being mustered into Company B, Indiana 1st Cavalry, 28th Regiment Volunteers. George signed on for three years of duty.

Evansville was a busy place, a real city on the Ohio River, not like the farm towns that Fly and George had grown up knowing. The streets were full of wagons and buggies, and there were people moving everywhere. Summers in Evansville are hot and steamy, and the air was thick with smells.

Fly lifted her nose and sniffed. She could smell the Ohio River, people cooking foods, the coal in the wagons that went past, and all the many horses and dogs.

The Ohio River makes a curve when it gets to Evansville, and that spot is known as The Crescent. Steam boats with big paddlewheels on the sides, or at the rear, went up and

down the river. High atop each boat, in the pilot house, the captain searched the river ahead for dangerous snags and sandbars. Snags, which are uprooted trees that have been washed into the river, could seriously damage the hull or paddle wheel of the boat. Passing over a sandbar could make the boat run aground. The wheel for steering the ship around these obstacles was huge, with knobby handles sticking out at the end of each spoke.

The levee on Water Street was where the town traffic met the river traffic. The bank was paved with brown cobblestones, and at the water's edge, wooden platforms floated. These floating docks were anchored to the bank, and boats would tie up to them, to load or unload crates, barrels and bales of things that people sent up and down the rivers.

19

Bridgette Z. Savage

The Wabash and Erie Canal came right into Evansville along Canal Street. Canal boats were long and not very wide, so that they could get past each other in the narrow waterways. Horses that walked along the tow path on either side of the canal pulled each boat with a long tow rope. Passengers and cargo could ride on the canals all the way from Albany, New York, to Evansville, and get on the riverboats that traveled the Ohio.

Further downriver, the Ohio joins the Mississippi, which goes all the way to New Orleans and the Gulf of Mexico. The water was like a highway that carried the steam boats, rafts, and boxy-looking flat boats with cabins on them far and wide.

Chapter Three
War

The South was using the great rivers for shipping out cotton and other produce to Europe, and the sale of these things brought in money and supplies for the Confederate government and army. The North, of course, wanted to block this flow of goods, and cut off the Confederate states so that the North could win the war. With the seacoast and rivers, there were 4,000 miles of shore line for the small Union Navy to patrol.

At sea, the Navy concentrated on the large coastal cities of Savannah, Georgia, Charleston, North Carolina, and New Orleans, Louisiana. By blockading New Orleans, supplies to the rebel troops along the Mississippi River would be cut off.

Iron clad boats, that sat low in the water, were used on the rivers to attack the Rebel forts and camps that fired cannons on the Union boats moving troops up and down the rivers. The ironclads could also ram and sink other boats in battles.

Michigan, Ohio, Indiana, Illinois were still new states, and the soldiers who came from there were needed to fight in the West to control the Mississippi River Valley.

President Lincoln knew the importance of the rivers, and had even helped take a flatboat from Indiana to New Orleans when he was just a teenager. Now Abe Lincoln had issued a call for volunteers after the big battles in the East had gone badly for the Union troops.

Thousands of young men were enlisting in the Union Army. All over the country, Army enlistment officers were writing down young men's names, the color of their hair and eyes, and other important details in large books.

Men could enlist in different branches of Army service. There was the infantry, who were foot soldiers; the artillery, which manned cannons in forts or on artillery wagons which traveled with the Army; and there were the mounted soldiers, called the cavalry. George and Fly joined the cavalry, of course.

Especially in the early part of the Civil War, the Southern Cavalry had an advantage over the North. There was a great tradition of horsemanship and riding skills in the South. Many plantations had fancy racehorses from registered bloodlines. Men who enlisted in the Confederate Army usually brought their own mounts with them. They formed a ready cavalry of experienced riders comfortable with their horses.

When cavalrymen from the Eastern states of the Union enlisted, they usually had very little riding experience, and were assigned to horses that they didn't even know. Sometimes the horses weren't in good condition, and men who were riding them had no idea how to take care of them. Later on, recruiting posters that were sent out in the North encouraged men to bring their own horses when they joined the cavalry.

After George and Fly reported to Evansville, they went on to St. Louis, Missouri, to do training camp. The boat ride down the river was exciting for both of them. The future seemed inviting, because they knew that this time of their life was a part of something that would make American history.

St. Louis was even more impressive than Evansville. Fly had never seen so many horses in one place at one time. The camp had buildings and tents for the men and horses, and a big field called a parade ground.

The saddles that the Army horses wore were very lightweight. The seat was a wooden frame covered with leather. It was called a "McClellan" saddle. There was no saddle horn, and no extra padding. McClellan saddles were made for the cavalry. They just had a belly-strap, or girth, to hold it on the horse. A blue wool saddle blanket went under it to protect the horse's back.

What cavalrymen carried with them was either strapped to the rider or the saddle. The cavalry saber, or sword, had

Bridgette Z. Savage

a blade as long as a man's leg, and was used in charges and close combat. It hung down at the rider's side, usually to the left, so that it could be drawn out with the right hand.

A cavalryman's guns would include pistols and a rifle, and their cartridges were carried in cartridge cases. Besides all of these things, there were saddle bags to hold the curry-comb, picket and rope for tying out the horse to graze, saddle grease, and other important things. Binoculars, canteens, and maps all had their straps, cases, and pouches, as well.

The saddle had slots and loops for attaching all of the pouches and straps. Tied in front of and behind the saddle would be the blanket roll and a thin, rubberized blanket to be used as ground cloth if the soldier had to sleep out in the open, or as a cover in a downpour of rain. Hanging down to one side of the back of the saddle was Fly's feedbag. When she was picketed out, George could put her oats in the bag, and hang the strap over her head, behind her ears, and she could eat her ration of feed.

Horses who are working hard need to have grain every day, and it was one of the important supplies that the supply wagons carried. Heavy supplies that the cavalry used were carried in the supply wagons. The wagons were safe in the encampments when the men went out on short missions, but for longer expeditions, the wagons were taken along.

The men were outfitted with their standard issue gear, and uniforms. Cavalrymen wore light blue pants, which were supposed to be on the outside of their high leather boots, not tucked in. Their jackets were short, ending at the waist, made of dark blue wool. They also had long, light blue wool overcoats for cold weather. The cavalryman's hat was called a forage cap, and had a short black leather bill, and a flat top that tipped forward. The insignia of the cavalry was two crossed sabers.

All of these things were issued to the men by the quartermaster. It was the quartermaster's duty to keep track of everything that the men used, and to keep ordering new supplies and getting them passed out. He was the supply sergeant for his unit. Everything that was issued to each soldier was written down in the book that the quartermaster kept with him. Volunteer units, like the one George and Fly were in, often brought saddle blankets and equipment from home.

In training, the men learned what the bugle signals meant: Which notes meant to "draw sabers", which signal meant to charge, and what the "retreat" signal sounded like. The drums, cymbals, and fife were used to keep time when marching, or in parade. They also learned how to use and take care of all of their equipment, including their weapons. Using the saber was a new skill for the men, because not many people used swords any more in 1863. As the soldiers practiced with the sabers, they had to learn to both attack the enemy and also defend themselves.

Fly liked the routine of training camp. She was a horse who liked to know the work that she was supposed to do, and then do it the best she could. On the farm, the schedule had been very regular, with the Barretts doing chores like clockwork. That's what it took to run a good farm.

Life in the training camp was also regular, and there was a lot of drilling. A drill is a practice, and what the calvary needed to practice was how to move as a group without running into each other or getting in the way of other horses and men. To do this, the horses and their riders went to a large, open field each day and walked, trotted, and galloped in different directions, as they were told to do by their commanding officer. Sometimes the whole group would move, and sometimes only small groups of the men and horses were supposed to move.

One day, Fly was waiting for the training drill to start, and watching the other men getting their horses ready. She wondered where her rider could be? He had never been late before, but the minutes passed, and she saw the men saddle up all of the other horses and head out to the parade ground. Where could George be? Fly was extremely upset! This was NOT how things were supposed to go!

Of course, even if the men would have told her that George had gotten sick, she could not have understood them.

Finally, as if deciding that she knew what she was supposed to do, even if no one else did, she broke free from the hitching post and hurried to catch up with the other horses. Finding her place in the line, she fell in with the other troops, and went through the entire drill with her company. When the line of horses turned, she turned. When it was time to halt, she stood straight and tall, with her head up and ears forward. Staying in position, she moved as smoothly as if her usual rider were mounted on her back.

When the drill was over, she stayed in line all the way back to the stables. Fly knew that she had done her job that day.

Chapter Four
Into the Iron Mountains

After about two months of training, George, Fly, and their regiment of the Indiana Cavalry went down into the hills of southeast Missouri. They were in the Iron Mountains. It wasn't very long before they had their first run-in with the Confederate troops.

Unplanned fights that break out when enemies meet each other are called skirmishes. In a skirmish, both sides may be surprised, and have to make split-second decisions about how to win or escape. It's not like a full-scale battle, where the commanding officers have time to study maps and make plans.

Skirmishes and ambushes were something that could be expected at any time, unless you were in a well-defended camp or town. Since the cavalrymen were used as scouts and foragers, they were often ahead of the other troops, and were the first to run into enemy soldiers.

Fly's first skirmish was at Fredricktown, on October 18th. It was the first close look at the enemy for Fly and George. Shots rang out. Hearts pounding, the soldiers returned fire

29

and took cover. The fight was short, with both sides evenly matched. After the Rebels withdrew, the Union soldiers returned to their camp. Suddenly, the war was real, and they knew that they were on dangerous ground. Just a few days later, Fly and George were a part of a real battle near the same place.

Fredricktown was an important foothold for the Rebel troops in southeast Missouri. If the Rebels could control the areas along the Mississippi River, then they could keep the Union army from attacking the Confederacy from the west. The Southern leaders wanted to concentrate their forces in the East, where they were moving closer to taking over the United States Capitol in Washington, D.C. Along the East Coast, the U.S. Navy was blockading the South's coastal cities. Everything was locked in a balance that both sides were trying to break.

On the 21st of October, Confederate General M. Jeff Thompson led his men and a wagon train out of Fredricktown to get supplies. Two columns of Union troops that included the 1st Indiana Cavalry were ready to move in. Colonel William P. Carlin and Colonel J.B. Plummer were in command of the Union troops. When Thompson's force was about twelve miles south, he left the supply train, and returned to the town. He found out that the Union forces had already arrived. Thompson spent the morning trying to size up how many and what kind of Union troops were in the town. By noon, he decided to attack anyway, even though he could not get a clear understanding of the enemy he faced.

The Union soldiers came out to meet him, and Thompson's men were so outnumbered that they began to retreat. The Union Cavalry chased the Confederate attackers away from Fredricktown. The battle had been won, and one more piece of southeastern Missouri was now in Union hands.

One thing that Fly knew for certain after that day: This job was going to be a lot different than what she learned in training camp. Knowing what to do on the parade ground was important, but knowing how to use it in the field was more important.

War is a hard thing to understand. The Civil War was especially hard to understand. Sometimes brothers were fighting on opposite sides, shooting at their own family members. George knew about the big ideas that the thousands of men were willing to give their lives to defend. Fly did not. Fly was in the war because she was with George.

George could be brave because he understood what was going on, and could think ahead about the maps and the orders that he had been given. Fly was brave because that's just how she was made. Fly had learned from her mother to trust and to work, and that's what she did.

A soldier knows that, when two armies start firing cannons at each other, there is the noise of their own cannons, and also the noise of the other army's cannonballs hitting and destroying things where the soldier is standing.

People understand that when the infantry starts shooting their rifles, there is all of the noise and smoke of their own fire, plus the sounds of bullets from the other army shooting back at them.

But from the point of view of a horse, it makes no sense at all. Things just start happening. All of a sudden, there is noise, the smell of gunpowder and blood, sounds of men yelling, then screaming in pain. Dirt, buildings and trees start shattering and pieces of things are thrown into the air. It seems as if the whole world is blowing up all at once. Bugles sound the charge, and men yell. Every survival instinct a horse has tells it to bolt and run away. A good calvary horse like Fly has to be able to run right into what scares them most. When the noise and fighting started, Fly had to do what George told her as he used the reins on her neck, and his knees on her ribs.

She also had to keep her own eyes opened for danger. Some Southern soldiers had long sticks with knives on the ends, called pikes. They might come up from the side and hurt her or George. If they could cut her bridle, or snag her reins, they could hope to make George lose control of Fly, and fall off. The infantry had sharp bayonets on their rifles to stab and cut enemy horses and men. Cavalrymen had swords, too, and could slash and jab at each other. Fly had to know how to charge at men on foot, or on other horses, to knock into them so that they couldn't hurt her or George. George had pistols, but so did the men that they were fighting.

Sometimes George would dismount to stand behind a tree and shoot. Fly had to stand where he left her, and not leave him. When they charged, or had to retreat from the enemy, Fly had to run over all kinds of ground, jump over stone or split-rail fences, and get through creeks and mud. A broken leg would be the end of both of them. Her neat black hooves carried them both through all sorts of places in all kinds of weather.

Horse's hooves are a hard, thick toenail that covers the outside of their foot. They are growing all the time, just like people's fingernails and toenails do. Hooves have to be trimmed and kept in shape, so that the horse can stand straight, and the bones of their feet and legs don't get bent out of line and twisted. If horses are going to be walking on rough, hard ground, they need to wear metal horse shoes. Blacksmiths, who work metal, and farriers, who shoe horses, traveled with the army outfits. The blacksmith also made and repaired all sorts of equipment and hardware for the wagons and harnesses. With his hammer and anvil, the blacksmith made everything from horseshoes to hinges. The ringing sound of his hammer could be heard all over the camp.

Missouri and Arkansas have the Ozark Mountains. The hills are rocky, with thin top soil, and the creeks are full of gravel. The clear water from the hills rushes over stream beds filled with chips of flint, chert, sandstone, and other rocks. Fly had grown up in the wide river valleys of Southern Indiana. She was used to the soft, sandy soil of Posey County. The crunching of gravel under her hooves was strange to hear and feel as she walked along the roads and paths of the Ozarks.

Gravel is hard on horses' hooves. Even a small pebble that worked into a crack in a hoof wall could cause a horse to go lame. If a shoe came loose, or didn't fit right because the hoof had grown, the farrier had to work on the horse's foot and fix the problem before it got out of hand. The old iron horse shoe was pulled off, so that the hoof could be trimmed and filed into shape. Then a new shoe was put on with long, thin horseshoe nails that went through the thick, hard part of the hoof wall. The sharp points of the nails that stuck out on the outside of the hoof were then nipped off with a pair of cutting pliers. Finally, a big file was used to smooth down the ends of the nails. The blacksmiths and farriers who traveled with the cavalry were kept busy in the rough hills of Missouri.

Chapter Five
Hazardous Travels

Friendships are built by sharing experiences, and by finding that you can always count on your friend, no matter what. Each member of a friendship needs to be the sort that a friend can rely on. The experiences of George and Fly include their part of the history of the Civil War, and although they were already friends when they enlisted, their adventures made their ties even stronger.

There were many battles of the "War of Rebellion", as the Civil War was called by the North. Fly and George were in more battles and skirmishes during their years in the Army than I can put into this book. They traveled up and down the river valleys, saving and destroying bridges, trying to take over some towns and defending others. The travels, times, and other people they met were all a part of George and Fly's life together during the war.

In this time of their lives, they were both young and daring. But there is more to the story of Old Fly and George Barrett than the battles they fought or the adventures they had. There is the faithfulness and friendship that they shared. Neither one of them would have survived without the other.

On the 7th of July, 1862. Fly and George had just spent their first year in the Army. They were in Arkansas, near a place called Hills' Plantation. The Union Navy hadn't been able to get up the rivers to deliver supplies for quite some time, and the camp was running low on many things they needed. The armies of both sides had to rely on their governments sending food and ammunition to them by road, river and rail.

Even the flat, dry bread called hardtack looked good if there was nothing else to eat. Each man was given ten pieces of hardtack each day, with whatever other rations were on hand. Now even the supply of hardtack was running low. If the supplies couldn't get to the men, then the men had to get to the supplies. Major General Samuel R. Curtis decided to move his men to Helena, Arkansas.

Confederate Major General Hindman tried to prevent this by skirmishing with the Union troops. The Confederates attempted to block them at the Cache River Bridge on July 7th.

Fly and the 1st Cavalry were in the troops that moved forward, and all of a sudden they were ambushed. Gunfire burst out beside them, and George and the Union soldiers turned their horses to face the enemy. Fly saw the whites of the other horses eyes flash in fear, and felt George's knees squeezing her ribs. She moved to line up with the other horses.

Before both sides were completely turned to face each other, the Confederates charged forward in a frontal attack. The Union was forced to retreat. Knowing that they had to regroup to meet the next wave of the attack, they got into position to defend themselves.

This time, Union men and horses were able to turn and face their enemy, and stop the Confederates. As they took their stand to fight, reinforcements arrived and the Union soldiers were able to chase the Confederates away. Warily, the victorious Union soldiers crossed the Cache River Bridge, and moved on toward Helena. Once they were settled in, the men enjoyed a good meal, and the horses were given fresh grain. At least they were someplace safe, and the commanders could plan their next move.

Especially in the Trans-Mississippi campaign, which were the battles that Fly and George took part in, there was a lot of swampy ground that had to be crossed. The bayous and swamps along the rivers could be sticky like honey, but smell much worse. In the spring thaws, the dirt of the roads was full of ice crystals each morning, and turned to slippery mud by afternoon. Fall rains drenched everything, and even good dirt roads became rutted with the wheels of the artillery and supply wagons that passed over them. If they stayed in a camp long enough, the ground became so trampled by the feet of men and horses that it turned to a powdery dust. When it rained, the dust made a pasty mud that soaked into the soldiers' clothes, tents, and bedding.

Roads were a problem. The whole point of them is to be able to get from "here" to "there", and traveling was definitely the line of work for which the cavalry was intended. Although cities back then had stone or brick streets, and some places did use gravel to improve their roads, most of the highways and byways were dirt. Sometimes the soggy spots were covered over with wooden planks.

Corduroy roads were one way to make a mudhole passable. First, young trees were cut down. Those with straight trunks, more than six feet long, worked best. The limbs were stripped off, and the brush spread over the mud where the

road would be. Then, the logs were laid side-by-side, across the brush. It would take hundreds of trees to make even one mile of roadway. The final result was a long, bumpy strip of road that looked like a piece of corduroy cloth.

For men in the supply wagons, it was a rough ride, but it was better than standing knee-deep in mud and trying to push the wagon. For a horse, the logs were a hazard. Until everything settled into the mud, logs could roll, and a horse's hoof might slip down into an empty space, and get bruised or broken. In very wet weather, logs might float right up from the roadbed, and leave a gap that could trip up a horse and rider, and break the horse's leg.

But Fly was as surefooted as any horse that ever lived. No matter what was asked of her, she would find a way to do her job. If her job was to balance on floating logs in the mud, then she would give it a try.

Fly was, indeed, an all-round horse. Not as fancy as some, nor as big as others, but smart, willing and able. Men can plan, but horses have to think on their feet. It was good for Fly and her rider that she had four good ones.

In their travels, Fly and George had to find ways of getting places. Sometimes rivers would be in the path. For this, the Army Corps of Engineers built pontoon bridges, which floated on top of the water. If there was a large wagon train of supplies, or many soldiers on a march, all the parts for a pontoon bridge were packed on the supply wagons. The parts could be put together when they needed to cross a river.

But Fly and George were often with smaller groups of soldiers moving from one place to another. If they could not go on the roads for fear of meeting the enemy, or the bridges had been destroyed, they just had to swim. Horses can swim pretty well, even with a rider. Their long necks help them

hold their heads above the surface in deep water. If the men could take a raft or boat, the horses would swim behind, on a lead line. Sometimes there would be ferries to ride, and sometimes they could wade shallow water. The men always tried to stay near their horses, and to keep their guns and cartridges above the water and dry.

Once they were out of the water, men and horses walked until they were dried off. The harness and saddle had to be cared for, so that the leather would not dry out and crack. Saddle dressing is a mixture of grease and bee's wax, and it had to be rubbed onto the leather to keep it soft. Her saddle blanket had to be completely dried before it went back on Fly's back, or else she could get sores that would hurt and take a long time to heal. Even when they didn't have to swim rivers, there were lots of regular things that George did to take care of Fly. Her hooves had to be cleaned with a pick, she had to be curried and fed, and kept tied to the picket line.

George combed burrs and stick-tights from her mane and tail with the big teeth on the end of the curry comb.

Blood-sucking ticks would often come out when the fine teeth of the comb ran over her hair, or else they could be picked off by hand. If they had spent time in the swamps, George would check both Fly and himself for leeches. Those nasty creatures were harder to get off than ticks.

George, like about everyone in the Indiana Calvary, had grown up with horses, and most of the men had brought their own. Good horsemen knew that they had to take care of their horses before they took care of themselves. George did all that he could to keep Fly safe and sound, but one time, they had to swim a river with ice floating in it near Greenville, Mississippi. The water was so cold Fly's legs were numb by the time they reached shore, and the cold soaked deep into her body. Even worse, they had to make camp that night before Fly had walked enough to warm up and dry off.

Fly came down with what the men called "lung fever". The damp cold and exhaustion brought on a chill, and Fly's lungs were congested. She felt hot all over, and when George pressed his ear to her ribs, he could hear the rattling sounds inside her lungs as she heaved for breath. Blankets and hot water were all the help he could give her, and it looked pretty bad for a couple of days. Her head was down, her eyes were dull, and her body shook with chills as she fought off the fever.

When she looked around, things didn't look right to Fly. Everything was blurry, and it seemed like the ground was moving. Fly knew that she had to stay standing, no matter how dizzy and sick she felt. Locking her knees and spreading her feet to steady herself, she stood with her legs braced, refusing to go down.

By the end of the third day, she was feeling better, and held her head up. Although she was still weak, Fly could

Bridgette Z. Savage

walk a little. George stroked her neck with his hand, talking to her softly. Strength was returning to her legs and neck. When he put his ear against her ribs, George could hear the air passing freely in her lungs, and in a few more days, she was able to relax as she stood with her head up and bright eyes looking around the camp. It had been a bad scare for them both, and George was more determined than ever to get them home safely. As long as he could take care of her, this mare was his.

Chapter Six
Camp Life

When an army captured a town, it might become their base of operations for awhile. Troops could also set up a field camp, which was like a tent city. One way or another, the army had to have water nearby, and be in a place they could defend from attack.

In summer, life at the base camp could be dusty and hot. To have some shade men cut small trees to make what they called "shebangs". A shebang is made out of poles tied together, and looks like a framework for a house. All of the limbs of the trees were cut off, and put up on top to make a roof. It was something like a porch that had no house attached to it. Horses could be tied in the shebang, or it could be used as an outdoor mess hall. If there was a big wind, or a horse that was tied to one of the poles decided to take off, then "there went the whole shebang."

Winter had its own set of problems to be solved or lived around. In cold weather, men would find ways to heat their tents. Some tents were large enough for several men to live in, and they would build a fireplace at one end, and stack up empty wooden barrels to make a chimney. The men used several kinds of tents. Wall tents were like roomy canvas houses but the short dog tents had space for only two men.

There was a pointy, tall type of tent called a "Sibley", which had its own cone-shaped little stove that sat in the middle. The men inside would sleep in a circle, with their feet in the center, near the stove.

When they were in camp for a long time, soldiers would whittle, play cards, write letters home, or draw and write in their journals. If there was time, the men would even build log cabins.

At night around the campfire, men sang songs. Fly and the other horses were tied to the picket line, shoulder to shoulder, and haunch to haunch. The voices of the men blended together as they sang. "Tenting on the Old Camp-ground", which was sad, "Wait for the Wagon", which was a happy, fast song, and "Home, Sweet Home." These were songs that they all knew, or learned from each other. Voices rising and falling together floated on the evening breezes. Stars twinkled in the sky, up beyond the leaves overhead. Smoke from the fire drifted up, away from the circle of light where men sat, around the campfire. These nights were like little islands of peace, when the sounds were of people shar-ing a thought, a feeling, and a hope for different times.

Newspapers sent sketch artists to battlefields to make drawings. Other artists back at the newspaper office used these drawings to make pictures that were printed in the paper. Illustrated newspapers were very popular, because people wanted to know what was happening in the battles that they heard about.

Also during the Civil War, photographers traveled in their own wagons with their equipment and assistants. Their cameras were big boxes on legs, and instead of film,

Bridgette Z. Savage

46

they used square plates of glass covered with photographic chemicals. Some were Army photographers, but some were independent, and traveled on their own.

We can still see photos taken by Matthew Brady, George Barnard, Jay D. Edwards, Alexander and James Gardner, Timothy O'Sullivan, and George Cook. Pictures that these photographers took show us what things looked like to the people who were there. In these photos, we see long-ago moments in time, stopped forever. History is full of stories of past events, but looking into the eyes of the soldiers in old photographs tells a personal story.

By early December of 1862, Fly and George were in Oakland, Mississippi. The steady push into the South was continuing, and Northern troops were slowly but surely making headway. As the year was ending, and 1863 approached, many people remembered that they had thought this war would be over in six months. In Washington, President Lincoln planned what to do next.

There were great leaders in both armies of the Civil War, men who could see ahead, and make clear-headed decisions. A leader who could plan and figure things out earned the trust of his soldiers.

Before a big battle, officers study maps, send scouts to find out what the enemy's strength is, and make plans for changes that might take place during the fight. Men are gathered together and told what to expect. Troops move to position before the battle begins, and strategy is planned. There are some advantages to knowing ahead of time what you will face in battle.

While both sides wait to begin an attack, there is an eerie stillness. Many men pray. Everyone waits for a signal from the commanding officer. At last, the trumpet sounds a command to charge, and the color guard with the flag leads the way onto the field of battle. Voices rise up in war-cries and are mixed with the sound of cannon, rifle and pistol fire. Horses and men scream in pain, fear, anger, and every other emotion that can be imagined. The din of battle covers any spoken or yelled order, and commanders must keep their eyes on the movements of enemy troops, listen for signals from the buglers, and watch the other commanders to know what course the battle is taking. Officers realize that the men trust them to know what has to be done next, no matter how hard it might be. If the leaders aren't prepared, their men pay a horrible price.

A battle can change in an instant. One side may run out of ammunition, or may be counting on reinforcements that don't show up. Bad maps can cause men to end up marching into quicksand. Changes like this were the things that leaders had to be ready to handle.

During battles, signal flags were used to tell groups of soldiers where they needed to go, or if there were enemy troops approaching them. Men of the Signal Corps sent messages by a code that was called the "wig-wag" system. Messages were sent by the way that signal flags were moved up and down or left and right. At night, the same left-right and up-down codes could be used with torches. The Signal Corps was an important part of the army, back in the days when there was no other way to get words across long distances.

Battles were like nothing that many of the men had ever experienced before. The feeling that it caused was called "Seeing the Elephant". In other words, a battle was something so big and strange, that you had to see it to believe it.

The excitement of winning, the sorrow of loosing, fear, the horror and grief of seeing others wounded or dead, all left the men exhausted afterwards. Many felt old before their time.

Even when they weren't in battle, Fly and George couldn't relax. Any time they were going from one place to another, there was always the risk that a lone sharpshooter could shoot at them, or they could run into a full-scale ambush. If they were taken prisoner, George would be sent to a prison camp, where he could die from disease and starvation, and Fly would find herself with a new owner, fighting for the Confederates. Of course, there was always the chance that they could just be killed outright.

Chapter Seven
1863

All through the winter of 1863, Union General Ulysses S. Grant had tried to find a way to take the city of Vicksburg, Mississippi. Vicksburg was the key to controlling the Mississippi River. What Grant knew, and what would keep the cavalry running up and down the rivers during the war, was that, in order to win, the Union had to control the rivers of the Mississippi Valley. If they could do that, not only would the South be separated from the territories to the west, the North could move troops and supplies all along the western edge of the fighting, and launch attacks against the cities of the South. Of course, the leaders of the South had no intent of letting this happen. And so the two sides struggled for control.

Grant had men digging canals to divert the mighty river so that Vicksburg would be cut off from the water. If his plan worked, then the Union could send troops and supplies wherever they wanted along the river, and not have to go past the cannons of Vicksburg. Grant had four different plans of how to cut Vicksburg off from the river. He tried them all, and none worked. So now, the last plan was to lay siege to the city. Grant would keep the city under attack, while preventing any supplies or reinforcements from reaching it. Eventually, the Confederates would have to give up and surrender the city. If someone was going to have to call it quits, it wasn't going to be General U.S. Grant. Grant was a leader who could see the larger picture than just one battle. He knew that the Confederates were using their railroads to move troops from one front to another. As long as the North was skirmishing along the edge of the South, Rebels would always be there to meet them. In order to win this war, the North would have to break right into the South, not just run along the edges. And that is what Grant intended to do. He would take Vicksburg one way or another. The first thing that needed to be done was to keep the Rebels from bringing in their re-enforcements on the railroads.

And so, Fly, George, and a group of the cavalry took off from their camp north of Vicksburg one early morning in May for a hard day's ride. Their mission was to destroy a bridge to keep trains from bringing more Confederates into Vicksburg. They started out early in the day, when the sky was getting bright, and the birds were singing. They kept riding as the sun got higher in the sky. Some horses can run fast, but only for a little while. Some horses can work all day, but only at a slow pace. Horses picked for this mission had to move fast and keep going until the job was done. Fly was that kind of horse. On and on they went. The sun was past the midpoint of the sky, and still they kept going. Fly kept up her steady pace, and the hours of the day slid past like the miles of the road under her hooves. They covered eighty miles that day before they reached their destination.

As they got closer, Fly could tell that they needed to hurry. There was a railroad ahead. Her ears could hear the

Bridgette Z. Savage

52

train, far away. Her nose could smell the coal smoke from the locomotive. Harder and harder they rode. Fly was tired. The men were silent. Yet, on and on they went. She could smell the river.

There was the bridge. The train was just crossing...the train full of Confederate troops headed towards Vicksburg.

The cavalry was too late. They had tried so hard, pushed so far. What could they do now? As the train rolled out of sight, they decided that no more Rebel soldiers would get to use this bridge. While Fly and the other horses rested, the men drug dry wood from the hillsides, and stacked it up against the wooden trestles. They set fire to the wood, and soon, the bridge was burning. Iron rails and spikes fell into the valley, and the bridge was destroyed. George and the men got back into the saddle, and rode another twenty miles before they found a safe place to make camp for the night.

It had been a hundred mile day. Fly could feel how tired she was as George climbed down to the ground. George ached, too. There wasn't much padding on a McClellan saddle. Although they were both tired, George knew he had to take care of Fly before he took care of himself. He uncinched the girth strap, and slid the saddle from her back. Next, the saddle blanket came off. He ran his hand along her back and down her smooth side. After he took off her bridle and bit, George rubbed Fly down and made sure she had food and water. The day of the long ride was over at last.

Later that same month, Fly and George were with a group from the 1st Indiana Cavalry that went to take Island 65 on the Mississippi River. The islands on the Mississippi River are numbered, starting at Cairo, Illinois, and going downstream towards the Gulf of Mexico. There had been a great battle with iron clad ships to take Island 10, near New Madrid. Island 65 was further south, so they were making progress. That day, they were with an Arkansas Regiment, led by Lieutenant Colonel George W. DeCasta, and some of the 36th Iowa Infantry. Many of the men with George and Fly that day were African-American soldiers. They were free men who had enlisted in the Union Army to fight for the North.

Using the steamboat *Pike*, they took a piece of artillery with them, and set off down the river. It was a strange day; on land, on boat, and on land again. Fly paid attention to getting on and off the boat. The gangplank was like a movable bridge between the deck and the muddy bank of the island, and not something that a nervous horse would walk on. With the men and horses attacking on land, and the cannon on board the *Pike*, the Union Army was able to attack from two different directions. The Confederates were surrounded, and defeated. Island 65 was under Union control.

During this spring, Fly and George got to see lots of places with interesting names, like Yazoo Pass, Mitchell's Crossroads, Grenada, Mississippi, and the Coldwater and Tallahatchie Rivers. With all of the miles they covered, it was a good thing for George that Fly was a smooth traveler, and a pleasure to ride.

Grant did finally take Vicksburg after a siege that lasted from May, 18 to July 4, 1863. The people of Vicksburg were living in caves that they had dug into the dirt, to protect themselves from the cannonballs and artillery shells. By the time the Confederates gave up the city, everyone was starving and rats were running everywhere.

George was twenty-two years old, and Fly was eight. They both felt like Indiana was some lovely dream that happened long ago, maybe to someone else. It seemed like much more than two years had passed since they were on the levee at Evansville, excited to be going away from home.

General Grant wanted to drive on into the South, now that Vicksburg was taken. But the armies were being sent to other areas, and even generals had to follow orders.

At the same time that Vicksburg was finally being surrendered, Fly found herself in the battle for Helena, Arkansas. In other parts of the United States, like New York, Indianapolis, and Chicago, people were celebrating the birth of American independence with fireworks. Deep in the hills of the river valleys, Union troops were fighting to put the nation back together.

Cities like Helena, Arkansas, were always targets for attack, and during the battle on July the fourth, Fly could hear the big sounds, like rolling thunder, dull thuds coming from the earth below her hooves. They were the shock waves of the cannon firing and the enemy shells smashing into the town. The Union troops were in Helena, and Confederate Lt. Gen. Holmes was attacking with more troops under his command than the Union had in town.

At first, it looked like the Southern soldiers would win. They had gained control of some of the fortifications at the edge of the city. If they could take over Helena, General Holmes knew, they could force the Union army to draw troops away from Vicksburg, and weaken the hold that the Union had on the South. The plan might have worked, but the Union knew what was at stake, and held on to their positions. In the end, the Confederate forces had to withdraw, leaving the city in Union hands.

By keeping Helena, the North would be able to launch a campaign on Little Rock. It was going to be a long, hard job to take the South, one piece at a time. The Rebels believed in their cause just as strongly as the Union believed in their own. Men of both armies felt that they were fighting to save their countries.

Chapter Eight
Bayous and Battles

It was September 10, 1863. Another autumn was on its way. On small farms, people were gathering in their crops from the fields and gardens. They were hiding away what they could, to keep it from being taken by soldiers from either side. The cavalry horses and men that Fly was with were on the move again. They were sent into the swampy wetlands called Bayou Forche', near Little Rock, Arkansas.

Bayous are like swamps, and back home in Indiana the rivers of Posey County had areas called bayous, so Fly had an idea of what they were like. It was best to stay out of them. There were snakes and snapping turtles that grew to enormous size. Sometimes the water was black from the stain of tree leaves. The ground could be dangerously soft, and muddy enough that a horse could get mired and stuck. Meeting up with an enemy under these conditions could be deadly.

In the middle of Bayou Forche', that's just what happened. The Union Cavalry ran into a group of Confederates. It looked like George and Fly's group were in trouble, pinned down in the swamp across the river from where they meant to be. They could not retreat from the Rebels, and there was no way to move forward.

Fortunately, the Union artillery on the north side of the river began to fire on the Confederates, who drew back. Fly and George's group of cavalry were able to advance as the Confederates retreated into Little Rock to escape the artillery fire. To reach the city, Fly and the other horses swam the Arkansas River. As the cavalry charged forward, the Union infantry and artillery moved in, and by the end of the evening, the Union forces had taken the town. Little Rock was no longer held by the Confederates. George picked dried mud out of Fly's tail that night, and brushed the last of Bayou Forche' out of her dark hair.

After that summer passed, another fall came. It was the end of October, 1863. Dried corn stalks were gathered up in shocks in the field. They were big bundles that looked like teepees in the twilight of evening. Colorful leaves skittered across dirt roads, and piled up along fencerows. Back home in Indiana, the harvest was in. Corn cribs were full, and pumpkins had been rolled into cellars for the winter. Sweet apple cider was being squeezed in the cider presses. In Posey County, families read newspapers to follow the war, and waited for letters that would let them know what had happened to their sons.

By then, Fly and George had moved to a city named Pine Bluff, in Arkansas. The Union held Pine Bluff, but the Confederates kept trying to take it over. That fall, Union Colonel Powell Clayton had two U.S. Cavalry regiments and a company of state militia stationed there. He sent out a company of cavalry towards the town of Princeton. They ran into Confederate General Marmaduke's soldiers, who were advancing on Pine Bluff. There was some shooting from both sides, then the Southerners waved a flag of truce.   Officers from both sides came forward, and the Southerners demanded that the Union forces surrender to them.   The Union had other ideas.   Colonel Clayton kept his men together, and slowly pulled back into the town of Pine Bluff.   Both armies spent the night getting ready to do battle the next day.

What George and Fly would remember years later was that, early in the morning, Confederates started shooting their artillery into the town.   Horrible explosions split the morning silence as buildings were struck by artillery shells. Women ran in the streets with their children, trying to find shelter.   Crying in terror, they begged the Union soldiers to tell them where to go to be safe.

Men rushing to their posts yelled for the women to move to the far side of town, and get down below the river banks, where the shells and rifle fire could not reach them.   Mothers ran through the streets carrying or dragging their children. They slid down over the muddy river bank like otters, desperate to get out of harm's way.   For hours, they sat huddled together, dirty and wet, while the two armies fought over who would control the town.

History books tell us that there was a lot going on in the town of Pine Bluff that day.   At one point, about 300 African-American soldiers from the Arkansas infantry rolled huge bales of cotton out of the warehouses in town, to use as barricades against the Rebel advance.

Cannon sounds rumbled in the air, making the streets of the town shake.   Fly felt the thuds of the big artillery shells hitting the ground.   Shock waves ran through stone and brick, and she felt the earth shake beneath her hooves.

When the Confederates couldn't drive the Union army out, they tried to burn down the town.   Smoke and embers stung Fly's nostrils as she galloped through the streets,

carrying George to block the Rebels from taking the buildings at the edge of town. Every time the Rebels tried to work their way in to the town, Union soldiers blocked their path. In the end, the Rebels decided that they couldn't take the city and gave up, leaving the wreckage of Pine Bluff in Union hands.

Dirty, tired families crept back to their homes, or what was left of them. As night fell, the officers sat up writing, making note of all that had happened in the battle, and who had been shot or killed. It was the officers' responsibility to record, for the Official Record, where every group of men had been in the battle. They especially needed the names of those who had died, so that letters could be sent to the families who would never see their soldiers come home.

Chapter Nine
1864

To move from battle to battle, the men and horses had to climb onto railroad cars, or riverboats, or just walk and swim their way to where their commanders said that they were needed. Many of the orders came as a letter that was carried by a messenger on horseback, but sometimes, they came by telegraph.

The telegraph was one of the new inventions in the 1860's. People had known about electricity for quite awhile, but the telegraph was one of the first ways found to put it to use. Rubber coated wires were strung from sapling poles, over bushes, and along the ground. The battery wagon had equipment to send an electrical current through the wire, and the telegraph operator used the "key" to send messages in Morse code. A telegraph key is a simple tool that taps the circuit open and closed, and Morse code is made up of "dots" and "dashes". A dot is a short key stroke, and a dash is a little longer.

It's hard to believe that there are people who can listen to the ticking sound of the incoming message, and change it

into words in their heads, but that's what telegraph opera-
tors learned to do. The enemy could "listen in", by hooking
their own keys to the line.

Because each side wanted to keep their information secret, they used "cipher wheels", which lined up different letters with the usual ones of the alphabet. A cipher wheel is
a tool used to change the words of a message into a code. A
person receiving the coded message needed to have another
cipher wheel to decode the message.

It works like this. There are two wheels with the 26 letters of the alphabet on them. The smaller wheel sits on top
of the larger one and the sets of letters line up with each
other. By turning one of the wheels, the letters are shifted
over and line up with different letters on the other wheel.

In order to send a message in code, words are spelled using the "correct" letters on one wheel, but written with the "shifted over" alphabet of the other wheel. The coded message appears as an unreadable assortment of misspelled words until the message is decoded. When a ciphered message came across the wire, the telegraph operator had to decipher it before it could be read. There was a lot of ticking and tapping involved in keeping messages going.

To Fly, the battery wagon with the men sitting in it was just another wagon in the supply train. No oats or molasses there, but it sure sounded like it was full of bugs.

At the end of March, 1864, Fly and George were at Mt. Elba, Arkansas. They didn't have much time to rest. By now, Union and Confederate forces were on the move, all the way from Arkansas down through Louisiana. The Union Army was trying to push through Arkansas and take over a part of Texas. This plan was called the Red River Campaign.

The War had been going on a long, long time. This constant moving from one place to another had become the usual and expected thing for Fly to do. As long as she was with George, she knew that she was doing what she was supposed to do. Winter was finally gone, and springtime had come again. Magnolia trees were opening their huge white flowers, and honey bees buzzed in the fruit trees.

In April, down in the hills of Arkansas, the leaves are coming out. With the young leaves filling in the branches of the trees, you can't see as far into the woods as you might in January, when the limbs are bare. That was probably both a good and a bad thing for Fly and George on this day.

There is an old saying that "An army travels on its stomach", which means that if they don't have food, they can't keep going. Supplies like hardtack, dried beef, dried apples and berries were shipped in barrels. Gunpowder, blankets,

Bridgette Z. Savage

even letters from home were necessary things that could only be delivered if the supply lines stayed opened. In war, just keeping the troops supplied was a risky job.

For one thing, it was difficult to get things safely up the river and to a landing where the army could send wagons to them pick up. In the North, there were still farms and factories working to make the things to keep the Union troops going. The Rebels would have loved to capture these supplies, because they were fighting a war on their own land, where the farms and plantations that their food came from were being destroyed. So if the Rebels could keep the Union soldiers from getting supplies, it was good for them in a couple of ways. Not only would the Union men and animals go hungry, the Rebels would have the supplies for their own use.

In fact, that's just what the Confederates had done near Poison Spring, Arkansas, less than two weeks before. An entire wagon train of supplies had been captured by the hungry Rebels.

Near the end of April, two hundred and forty wagons left Camden, Arkansas, headed towards Pine Bluff to get supplies. The wagon train, with artillery, troops and horses, was two miles long. Among the cavalry and infantry forces escorting the supply train were Fly and George.

As the long convoy crept cautiously across the Arkansas landscape, Confederate forces attacked them. At first, it seemed as if the cavalry and foot soldiers could drive off the Rebels. But soon the Confederates divided into two groups and attacked both the front and the rear of the supply column.

The Union soldiers were spread too thin, trying to protect both ends of the wagon train at once. There was no escape. All of the wagons were captured on the road, and most of the men, as well. The Union Commander, Lt. Col. Francis Drake, yelled the order for his men to get away if they could.

Fly, George, and twenty-seven other cavalrymen escaped together, but as they headed in one direction, a group of Confederate soldiers cut them off.

The cavalrymen turned quickly, and took off in another direction. More Confederates! Knowing that there was no point in going back to the road where the captured wagons were, they made a break towards a nearby river. Hoping that there was still a gap between the two groups of Confederates, the men ran their horses through the woods. If they could get across the river, then there just might be a chance of making it to either Pine Bluff, or back to Camden without being killed or captured. Fly ran like the wind, with tree trunks flashing past on either side of her. As George hunched down low in the saddle, he caught glimpses of the other men racing through the woods.

Staying together, the horsemen dashed toward the river. They knew it must be ahead of them. The woods were thinning out, and the sky shone through the tree branches ahead. Bursting out from the shelter of the trees, their hearts almost stopped as they reined in the horses. The wild escape from the Confederates had led right to the edge of a giant drop-off. They were stranded on a high bluff. Looking over the edge, it was plain to see that the river was deep at the foot of the cliff. There was no way to slide down the steep bank, and no other way to escape.

As they talked, a desperate plan came together. It was a long way down to the water below, too far for each rider to stay on his horse as it jumped in. The cliff was too high for the horse to even want to jump in! The men decided that the horses would have to be pushed off the edge, and then the rider would jump, and try to keep up with his horse as it crossed the river. Hopefully, each man would reach the other side in time to catch his mount. Two men who were sure that they could swim the river volunteered to be last, in order to get all of the horses off of the cliff. With luck, the men who had already made it across could catch the last two horses and hold them until their riders reached the shore.

The first horse was brought up to the edge. With one man on either side, the men locked their arms behind the horse, as its rider worked to keep the horse's head and shoulders pointed in the right direction. The men behind the horse pushed forward and shoved it over the edge. The rider went over the brink with his horse. With a huge splash, they hit the water. It was so deep that both horse and rider disappeared from sight for a moment, then bobbed to the surface. Horse and rider after horse and rider took the plunge and swam for the far shore.

When it was Fly's turn, she surely must have thought that, of all of George's ideas so far, this one was the strangest yet. Before either one of them had time to think, they were both falling through the air. George hit the water at almost the same time as Fly. The breath-taking fall ended with cold water all around them. In the split second that they hit the water, all natural sound stopped. Both Fly and George were surrounded by swirling bubbles and the strange sound of water in their ears. Then they popped back up to the surface. Fly started swimming immediately, and George managed to grab hold of her tail. He knew that they had to get out of the way of the next man and horse coming off the cliff, or they might get hit. Fortunately, the river current had carried them downstream a little, so that they were safely away as they heard the next big splash in the water behind them. Fly towed George across, and they waited with the others on the far bank.

Water dripped from the men and horses as they stood silently among the trees of the far riverbank. Their wet, cold uniforms stuck to their skins, and their boots were full of water. Their friends looked small and far away at the top of the bluff across the river. The only sound, aside from the splash of horsemen and horses hitting the river, was the horses' breathing and shaking the water from their manes. Nervously, the men watched. It seemed like hours before the last two men jumped from the cliff. Finally, everyone who had escaped was on the safe side of the river. Twenty-eight soaking wet men and horses started off for the Union camp. They were relieved and thankful to have escaped. At the same time, they were full of regret.

The wagon train was gone. They had no supplies to bring back, their cartridges and guns were wet, and hundreds of their fellow soldiers had been captured. It was a horrible defeat for the Union. Two supply wagons had been captured in less than two weeks. Hundreds of Union men would be sent to prison camps. The Union soldiers were low on supplies, and the wet spring weather was setting in.

After they reported back to camp, Union General Steele decided to retreat from Camden and pull back to the city of Little Rock. This was the only way that the battered Union Army could keep from starving to death or being captured. All of their equipment and supplies were packed into their remaining wagons. On the morning of April 26, General Steel and his men left Camden. By the next day, the Confederates had taken over the city and were hot on the trail of the retreating Union Army. If they could catch the fleeing Northerners, there was a good chance that the entire Union force could be destroyed.

For three days, Fly, George and the Union forces moved as fast and hard as men and horses could be made to move. They were running for their lives towards Jenkin's Ferry, where the Saline River could be crossed. Rain had been falling almost constantly, and the low land along the river was flooded. The infantry men had to march in knee-deep water, and wagons became stuck in the mud. They were moving slowly in a swamp filled with giant trees, with a Confederate force about to overtake them.

The situation looked grim for the Union troops, but General Steele had a plan for crossing the swollen river to safety.

Packed in the wagons were the parts of a new invention: an inflatable pontoon bridge! Instead of boats to hold up the walk-way of the bridge, this new type used rubber-covered canvas floats that were inflated like giant balloons and fastened together with rubber cords.

On the river bank, the men struggled to pump air into the floats and anchor them in place. The rain kept falling. The Confederates kept getting closer. Finally, the parts of the bridge were together and one wagon at a time began to cross the Saline.

By eight o'clock that morning most of the wagons had crossed the bridge. The Confederates caught up with the men guarding the rear of the wagon train and the fighting began. General Steele sent all of the men that he could back up the road to hold off the Confederates so that as many wagons as possible could cross the bridge.

Gunsmoke and fog mixed together until the soldiers could only see flashes from the musket barrels as they shot at each other. On the bridge, one wagon at a time slowly crossed. For six hours, men of both armies fought and died in the swampy woods. The horse soldiers galloped through flooded fields carrying boxes of fresh cartridges to the infantry. The infantrymen used their bayonets to pry open the boxes, and kept shooting.

At last, the Union troops had the river between themselves and the Confederates. General Steele ordered the men to slash the pontoon floats and cut the bridge loose from its anchors. As the bridge broke apart and drifted downstream, the Confederates had no way to follow the escaping Union Army.

Many wagons were stuck in the swampy ground on the north side of the river. General Steele ordered the men to burn the wagons and the supplies that were in them to keep them from being used by the Confederates. He took what was left of his army and headed for Little Rock.

Eight hundred men had been killed or wounded at Jenkins Ferry. The dead were left in the swamps.

George, Fly and the other survivors of the Red River Campaign arrived in Little Rock, Arkansas on May 3rd. Tired and hungry, they could only wonder what would happen to them next.

Chapter Ten
The Unlucky Ones

For the men who were captured in battle, there was the grim future of the prison camps. Prison camps on both sides were places where a soldier was likely to die of disease or malnutrition. Some were better than others, but none were places where you would choose to go.

Even when soldiers weren't captured or killed, being wounded in battle was a terrible thing. If a soldier were wounded, they might try to stop the bleeding themselves by wrapping a shirt or kerchief around their wound. When lines were being over-run by the enemy, a wounded man's friends may try to drag him to safety, if they could.

Injured men who could be moved off the battlefield were helped by non-combat military, like the drummers and supply runners. The lucky ones would be treated by a field doctor, who would find room on an ambulance wagon for them to be taken to a place from where they could be shipped to a hospital.

Back in the middle of the 19th century, even doctors didn't know about germs and how diseases were spread.

There were a few medicines that they could give to injured men for pain, if arms and legs had to be amputated, but nothing that could prevent infection from the wounds. No one was vaccinated against any diseases, and if one man in camp came down with something that others could catch, they did. For every one man killed in battle during this war, two others would die of illness.

Some very determined doctors and nurses like Mary Ann Bickerdyke, Dorthea Dix, and Clara Barton worked to improve hospital conditions. Army hospital ships, like the *Red Rover*, and hospital trains with special cars took injured soldiers from both armies to large, regular hospitals for care and recovery.

Injured horses, however, were another matter. Cuts and gashes could be stitched up, and ointment or tar smeared on the wound. If a horse went down on the battle field, men would crouch behind it for cover, using its body as a shield from enemy fire. If a horse broke a leg, there was nothing to do but shoot it to put it out of its misery. The rider would take the saddle and bridle, and start searching for a replacement.

Bodies of men were drug from the field and buried, or stones at least heaped up on them where they lay. The bodies of horses were sometimes just left to rot, or covered with brush and rails from fences, and burned.

This was all a part of the smell of a battlefield. Gun powder, burnt flesh, mud, and all. Whether your side won or lost, the smell of war was the same.

Once in awhile Fly would remember the clover and clean straw in the barn where she had lived before the war. It was very far away now, in both miles and memory. Her job now was not to plow, plant, and harvest. There were no hay wagons to pull, no loads of corn to take to the corn cribs. Her

job was to do her best to get George and herself through all these unusual things that kept happening. She had no idea what this was all about, but it certainly kept her busy.

All of the fields smelled of war. When Fly saw draft horses pulling cannons along the roads, she could smell the sharp scent of gunpowder clinging to the iron. Even the artillery soldiers themselves smelled of gunpowder.

As they rode past farms and towns, Fly saw things she'd seen before, but they were broken now. Fly could tell things were changing. Everything was worn out, used, and dirty.

The Confederate soldiers did not look and smell the same as at the beginning of the war. The South had always had more men in homespun uniforms than the North, but now, as the war drug on, the South's supplies were stretched even further. Men wore patched clothes and used all sorts of equipment. Some were using the old muskets that fired round balls. Although these guns were harder to shoot, some Rebels were excellent sharp-shooters, and the "minnie balls" were just as deadly as a rifle bullet, if they found their mark. A few of the Rebels didn't even have shoes. Their faces were hardened with determination.

Even the land was different than when they first came here. It was a battleground now. Battles may be planned, but the ground was meant to be used for something else. Generals move troops around, and try to force their enemies to meet them in places that are to their own advantage. People will plan battles to happen at times and places that will make it easier for them to win.

But battles are fought along roads, in ditches, on hill-sides, valleys and in towns. When farmers clear the trees and rocks from a field, and plow the soil, they are working to make things grow and live. Stones are stacked at the edges of fields to get them out of the way of the plow, and to make fences. People who make stone fences never plan for riflemen to crouch behind them and try to kill other people. Families that sit together around the lamp-light reading of an evening never imagine their home used as an army head-quarters, or destroyed by cannons.

Across the South, as the war began, America was cov-ered with farms, hemmed in with split-rail and stone fences. Families had worked long, hard years to clear the land, plant orchards, build root cellars, homes, and barns. Planting and harvesting crops was the work of most of the people. The railroads and ships took farm produce to distant markets, and brought goods back to the towns that dotted the maps. People in the North and the South had worked hard to make good homes for their families.

By the end of the war, there were homes with no fami-lies, and families with no homes. There were dead soldiers of both armies buried in unmarked graves. Bullet holes can still be seen today in farmhouses that just happened to be in the way, when that farm became a battleground.

President Lincoln had issued the Emancipation Procla-mation in the fall of 1862. It set the slaves in the Rebel states free as of January the first, 1863. This, by itself, would destroy the South's way of life.

George and Fly had been on duty in Missouri, Arkansas, Louisiana, and Mississippi. They never imagined that they would travel so many miles, or see so much. Some of the men and horses that they had been serving with were sent other places, to be parts of different campaigns and battles.

George and the other volunteers had signed on for three years. They were in Arkansas when the three years was over. To all the men and horses, much more than three years had passed since they set out on this adventure. But, as time is measured, it had only been three years. George's enlistment was over. Cavalrymen were told to report to Pine Bluff, Arkansas to be released from duty. George and Fly had a long trip ahead of them in order to get back to their home in Posey County.

Chapter Eleven
The Long Road Home

George was happy to know that they would be going home. He would soon see his family. He could listen to the crickets outside his bedroom window at night and watch the lightening bugs drifting over his family's hay fields. He would be able to walk down a road without being shot. All of the fear and loneliness that he had been holding inside seemed like a cloud that could be blown away by the wind.

If he and Fly could just get out of here safely, they would be on their way home soon. George had no desire to see more of the countryside than he had already seen in the last few years.

In Pine Bluff, George and the other men reported to the officers in charge to fill out paperwork. As George was giving his information to the man taking notes, the quartermaster was looking over the horses. The war was still going on, and no one knew when it would be over. The Union needed horses, and experienced ones like Fly were especially valuable.

The government was giving as much as $85.00 or even $100.00 for good horses. The quartermaster walked over to

George. He began talking about what a good horse Fly was. He told George the Army would pay $150.00 for Fly.

George was shocked.

In 1864, $150.00 was a large amount of money. It was enough to buy all sorts of things, or quite a bit of land. But it was not enough to buy Fly. He had never even considered going home without his friend. She was his. He'd done all that he could to keep her safe.

George knew that, after all that they had been through, they must both go home. He could not stand the thought of returning home without her. Could he convince them to let him keep Fly? And if he did, how could he get her back home?

It was too far to walk. And too dangerous. Arkansas and Missouri were still full of Rebels. As close as he could figure, they were about 400 miles from home, as the crow flies. Who knew how far they would actually have to travel as they zig-zagged their way north? Alone, traveling with Fly, he would be an easy target. They were in the middle of the South, surrounded by wrecked farms and towns, where Union soldiers were not welcomed. If they traveled on their own, they wouldn't have the supply wagon. No food, no supplies, no protection.

Even if the war was over soon, defeated men and their families would be walking the roads to try to find their way back to their own homes. Many would be angry and dangerous. George knew what he had to do.

George looked for and found Captain Bingham and Colonel Owen. Like George and Fly, these two officers were from Posey County, Indiana. George hoped that they could help him get home with Fly. He explained that Fly had always been his horse, and that he had raised her on the family farm. He needed her to work on the farm.

The two officers listened to him. Looking at Fly, and looking at George, they knew that they weren't going to change this young man's mind. Together, they agreed to help him, "As far as our authority goes", they said. They were just in charge of the land that their own troops were holding, so they could only promise to get him to the north edge of their own area.

Soon George had handwritten orders in his pocket. The paper only gave him and Fly passage to the next city, but at least it was a start. And so the first step of the trip home was a steam boat ride from Pine Bluff to Little Rock, Arkansas. George led Fly up the gangplank, and on to the boat that would take them up the Arkansas River to Little Rock.

As they walked onto the boat in Pine Bluff, it was strangely like the day they stepped off the dock in Evansville. Except, this time, George knew where they were going. George and Fly were on their way home to Indiana.

Back in the days of the Civil War, there were no gasoline engines. Paddle wheelers, like the locomotive trains, were powered by steam engines. These river boats were like big, flat barges that didn't set very deep in the water. As long as the water was two feet deep, the big boats could keep from dragging on the bottom of the river.

The river channels are constantly changing, and tons of silt and mud slide along the bottom, settling in different places each year. To keep from running the ship aground, the crew used long poles to check the depth of the river when they got into shallow water. The poles had marks every foot, and when the crewman called out "mark twain" it meant that the water was two feet deep.

Boats would take on coal at a river port, like Memphis or Cairo, and the coal would be shoveled into the firebox. Heat from the burning coal caused the water in the boilers to make steam, which ran the machinery that turned the big paddlewheels. All the way up the river, men would shovel coal, and the big wheels would turn. Twin smokestacks would puff out coal smoke, and the captain would pull a cord to sound a bell or steam whistle as they came into or left each stop.

When the steamboat reached a port, it would pull up along the wharf, and the crew would use strong ropes to moor the boat. Gang planks would be lowered, and passengers could load or unload. Workers took off or loaded on barrels of pork, sugar, flour, dried apples, giant bales of cotton, and everything else that was being shipped up or down the river. Horses, cows, pigs, and other livestock were walked on board and penned on the main deck. The boiler deck was the "upstairs" deck, where there were ship's cabins, which were individual rooms. The boiler itself was really on the main deck. The hurricane deck was the top deck, where the passengers went to enjoy the breezes. The texas deck was the top-most set of cabins, where the crew bunked. High above all was the pilot house, where the captain steered the ship. When they were ready to take off again, the captain would sound the whistle.

George was free to explore the ship, and hear news from the other passengers. There was a lot to talk about and share. Passengers asked each other where they had been, what they had seen. Even though the newspapers had descriptions of the war, people were anxious to hear personal, eye-witness accounts of the places that they longed to see. Soldiers were careful about what they said, because there were spies from both sides trying to gather information.

Fly, meanwhile, was enjoying her ride. During the war, she had swum across many rivers, including this one. It was a nice change to see so much water pass by without having to get wet. Trees and greenery on the banks slid past like clouds in the sky.

The two friends were on their way to civilian life again. They had traveled on the river boats before, when the iron-clads and armored gun boats were a common sight on the river. The War had ruled every part of life. But now there was something to think of besides war. It had been so long since anyone had been able to make plans past the next battle. Now there was a future to think about. It seemed like a long time since that had happened. There were still battles to be fought, and cities to be captured. Surrender by the South was a long way off, but George and Fly had done their part.

As George watched the river roll by, and the big wheels made the boat crawl north, he wondered what he'd do when he got to Little Rock. He'd have to find someone to help with the next leg of their journey.

As he listened to the talk of the other men, and passed places he remembered, he knew that it would be a long time before the regular business of life was put in order again. The only organization was the Army. He knew he must find the officers in charge as soon as the boat docked. In Little Rock, he led Fly down the gangplank onto solid land, and went straight to the Army officers who were in charge. Once again, he told his story, and explained how he would not leave his horse behind in the South. He showed them the papers he had gotten from the officers in Pine Bluff. The officers agreed to help him, and said that there was a train he could take, with Fly, to DeVal's Bluff, Arkansas.

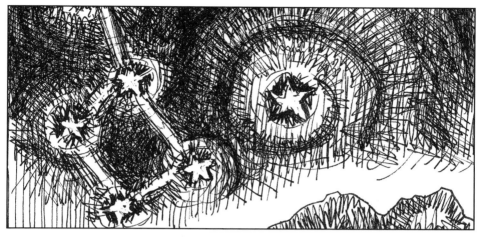

Chapter Twelve
Getting North

And so they took the train.

George rode Fly up to the rail road station, and talked to the people in charge, showing them his newest set of papers. Fly was loaded into a stock car, George got into one of the passenger cars, and the crew in the locomotive engine began to shovel coal from the coal car into the firebox. The boiler built up a head of steam, and the hollow banging sound of the steam pressure in the pipes grew louder and louder. As the engine's pistons started to move, the engineer sounded the whistle and they started off.

The train rocked on the tracks with a clicking and clacking as the big metal wheels rolled on the rails. As they chugged along, coal smoke rolled back over the cars, and off into the wind. The hills and fields sped past the windows as George and Fly left more of the South behind.

The Army officers at DeVal's Bluff told George that there was a steamboat taking troops north to Memphis, Tennessee. They gave him permission for passage on that boat, and to take Fly along with him. He added those papers to the ones that he already had, and rode Fly towards the landing. If he could just get them as far as Memphis, thought George, he'd figure out the rest of the trip from there.

Memphis was closer to home than he had been in three years. Tennessee was a lot closer to Indiana than Pine Bluff, Arkansas.

As he watched the banks of the river slide past, smoke from the smokestacks drifted off across the sky, and he thought of the many miles he'd traveled in the last few years. He felt better now. He was certain that, even if no one would help them after Memphis, he could ride Fly back home from there. After all, they would just have to travel a couple of hundred miles up river, between Tennessee and Arkansas, past Kentucky and Missouri, get around the end of Illinois, and they would be home again in Indiana. George knew that they could do it.

The Mississippi River drains the entire center of North America. From the Appalachian Mountains in the East, across the Great Plains, all the way out to the Rocky Mountains in the West, rivers flow into the Mississippi and the water heads towards New Orleans. It is called the Mighty River, and is a mile across when it reaches the delta. It's easy to follow, and hard to miss. As long as Fly and George were on the water, and headed upriver, they were on the way home.

In Memphis, George got passage for them on a steamboat all the way to Cairo, Illinois. The stack of papers in his pocket was growing.

At night, sounds of water on the boat hull lulled Fly to sleep. Overhead, stars shone in the sky. Up above the treeline, one special star was shining. It was the North Star, the one that the end of the Big Dipper points towards. It is the star that runaway slaves had followed to freedom since-

before the beginning of this war. Now, Fly and George were following it home.

On her forehead, Fly's white star shone in the moonlight. The night wind on the water played with her mane. She gave her tail a lazy swish, and shifted her weight. She'd been doing a lot of moving while standing still these last few days as the steamboat worked its way up the Mississippi River.

The boat passed Island Ten, Missouri and was soon docked in Cairo, Illinois. Fly and George were once again in the North. George got them onto another boat, this one heading up the Ohio River to Evansville, Indiana.

Getting ever closer to home, the two weary travelers followed the river upstream between Illinois and Kentucky. Finally, Indiana was on their left hand side.

It's funny how the land on both banks of the river looks the same, unless you know that your home is on one side, and not on the other.

At last, their boat rounded the Crescent at Evansville where their adventure began. Back on the levee with the brown cobblestones, George and Fly noticed that not a single building had cannonball holes in it. Aside from one visit by Morgan's Raiders, the Confederates had not come in to Indiana.

George found a livery stable where he could board Fly. The next leg of the trip for George was getting to Indianapolis. He had paperwork to take care of, and his discharge papers had to be signed. He felt that it would be safer for Fly to stay in Evansville. She was his horse, and they'd been through a lot. He didn't intend on having anything happen to her now.

There were other horses boarded at the stable. It was strange for Fly to stay in one place without George, and not be moving.

Fly noticed that, in Evansville, there was no sound of war. There was no smell of the battlefield. The boys who worked at the stable looked over the top of the stall at Fly. She looked up at them, remembering that people came in smaller sizes than the men that she had lived with for three years. The boys tried to see her scars, and told each other stories that they had heard about the war.

They gave her sweet hay. Good oats. Fresh water, without the taste of mud, gunpowder, and death. Things were different here, she could tell. But now what ? Was all of this traveling happening just to get to some new battle?

Somehow she didn't think so....

There was a breeze through the open window.

Long ago...it reminded her of a place long ago.

A place that she had known before the noise. Before the bugles and the explosions.

As for George, he was in the State Capitol, Indianapolis. It was a busy place, and there were many, military men there. There were men from different regiments, who had reached the end of their enlistment. Finding his way around town, George was relieved to see a city going about its daily routine, with shop keepers and markets opened for regular business. Men, women, and children went about their lives. Horse-pulled trolleys carried people from place to place. Buggies and wagons traveled freely in the streets.

It was almost a week before George was back in Evansville. Walking down the street, with his discharge papers in his pocket, he felt like he was on his own again. Now he had to face only the daily dangers of civilian life. No gunshots, no snipers, no horrible surprise ambushes. His life was for him to build. The nights around the campfire seemed long ago, and the camp songs seemed to have come true. George and Fly were going home at last.

He went to get some dinner, made sure that Fly was fed and watered, brushed and curried.

The curry comb ran over Fly's back. Her beautiful, straight, strong back. Her battle scars were healed over, but George could feel them as he ran his hand along her side. George had ridden Fly all over the map. She'd done her best, in blazing sun and through freezing rivers. He checked her hooves. Strong and hard. They had walked surefooted on corduroy roads, stood firm on the decks of steamboats, clomped across the floating pontoon bridges, slogged through swamps and bayous, been steady aboard the stockcars that rocked along the railroad tracks. And now they would carry them both home.

The blanket, the saddle, the belly strap. The bridle and the bit.

They set out on the road at about 1:00 in the afternoon. It was June, headed for July. They were going northwest, so the afternoon sun was on the left, and their shadows were on the right. Corn was almost knee-high in the fields they passed. Wheat was turning golden in the sun, and the wind sent ripples across the fields.

In fencerows, raspberries ripened, and trumpet vines bloomed, the same as they do when June comes around nowadays. No one was trying to shoot them. There were no ambushes laying in wait for them. They could just walk down the road, and be free. None of the farm houses that they passed had bullet holes in them. George let Fly use her smooth walk that carried them along at an even pace. Her shadow slid along beside them on the road, just like the shadows of the clouds on the rolling fields.

As they got closer to home, Fly became more excited. She lifted her head. Her nostrils flared as she breathed familiar smells. Her ears were straight up. Everything about her became alert. No, they were not going to a battle. There would be no shooting, no smoke, no death and screaming. Now she knew where they were going. It had been years since she had been there. But she knew.

This soft tan soil was ground that she had walked before. The fields were ones that she had plowed. The corn, oats and beans that grew here were the ones she had grown up eating. This was the ground that had grown her.

In battle or skirmish, Fly had always done exactly what George had told her. No matter what was going on, she would never bolt and run. She would go where his knees, hands, and voice told her to go, and never flinch or turn aside. But now, it didn't matter what George thought. Fly was taking them home, as fast as she could. George had felt joy when he knew he was headed home at last. Now it was Fly's turn to have that feeling. She had no idea what those papers that George carried meant. But she knew the meaning of these things around her.

The smell of home: June apples giving off their cider-scent under the trees, good soil with growing things, not rotting things, fresh water flowing in the creeks. She knew these things. This was the real news that the War was over for Fly. It was the promise of life going on. It was like an explosion of happiness inside her, and she took off at a run.

The closer they got to the Barrett Farm, the faster she went, until it was all that George could do to hang on. He put his weight in the stirrups and leaned forward. Fly started to whinny as they passed the maple trees before the gate. Her voice was like a high, loud laugh—a glad hello and hurrah!

At the farm, the Barrett family had no idea that George would be coming that afternoon. They heard Fly's whinnies and hoof-beats on the road, and rushed to the yard. All the thoughts they may have had about what this reunion would

be like were pushed aside by the grand entrance that Fly and George made.

Racing past the amazed Barretts, Fly ran straight to the barn, to her stall. Her own sweet walls and window. Where the hay smell, and the grain smell, and the other animals of the farm were alive, alive, alive.

And she knew that this is where she would live now, and for the rest of her time.

Fly was now nine years old. She and George had been in the Union Army for three years, and two months. She had been wounded three times, survived all sorts of weather from ice and rain to scorching sun. Disease and danger had been all around them for most of their service. They had seen more death and destruction than anyone could have imagined since they had last been on the homestead. George did the job that was given to him. He fought the war. Fly had done the job that was given to her. She had brought them both home safely.

In the North, the men like George who were lucky enough to return home could look forward to picking up where they left off. The fields were planted, and needed care. Sweet corn was growing in the garden and would soon be ripe. Watermelon vines were blooming, promising sweet fruit.

The Civil War went on for almost another year. That fall, Abe Lincoln won the election, and looked forward to being president for another four years. Through November and December, General Sherman led his Union forces to the destruction of Atlanta, Georgia, and marched on to the sea.

The South would take a long, long time to recover from all that had happened.

Chapter Thirteen
1865

The famous Confederate General Robert E. Lee surrendered his Army at Appomattox on April 9th. Abe Lincoln was assassinated five days later. Lincoln's funeral train came west to bring his body to its resting place in Springfield, Illinois.

In just five years, the United States had split into two countries, been reunited, had a president assassinated, doubled in size, and run head-long into a new age of factories, fast changes, and modern ways.

Even farming was changing. Big threshing machines, run by a steam engine, could thresh out more wheat in a half-day than a crew of men could do in a day by hand. Factories were making riding plows, hay mowing machines, and all sorts of things that made life easier and more productive.

Fly wasn't quite the same horse that she had been before the war. She had learned a lot of new things in her travels. George wasn't the same man, either. None of the young men who came back from battle were the same as they had been.

The world had changed, and so had they. Some men who had been in the cavalry took their horses and went adventuring, out to where the territories of the Wild West were still open. There were men who could never settle down, after all that they had seen and done.

Riverboats were bringing men back as quickly as possible. The *Luminary*, the *Henry Ames*, and the *Olive Branch* were some of the boats that were carrying happy crowds back home. George knew that he had been among the lucky ones, who were able to return home safely.

In April, while the country was still in shock about President Lincoln's death, there was the disaster of the *Sultana*. The *Sultana* was a paddlewheeler taking Union soldiers back north, to their homes and families. Many of the men had been prisoners-of-war at Andersonville prison, in Georgia, and were so weak that they could hardly walk. Instead of the 700 that might have usually gotten passage, there were close to 2000 people crammed on the ship.

As the Mississippi River rose to flood stage, the overloaded ship struggled against strong currents. The steamboat was having boiler troubles all the way upriver, and was forced to make repairs at Memphis, Tennessee. The *Sultana* left Memphis late at night on April 26th, and less than three hours later the people in Memphis heard the boilers explode. Rescuers set out in boats to help, but the *Sultana* was a burning wreckage. Over 400 Indiana men were injured or died that night. Many of them had been cavalrymen. They had been on the way home, and never made it.

During the war, George and Fly's regiment had lost four officers, and 32 enlisted men. Three officers and 148 enlisted men died because of disease. In all, 187 men from George's regiment who had met the call to arms would never come home.

Bridgette Z. Savage

With all that could have happened to them, it was hard to believe that Fly and George had gotten through it together. But they had. Part of it had to be luck, but part of it was that they were always looking out for each other.

On the Barrett's homestead farm, Fly's life was full of the regular farm work that she had known in the first six years of her life. On most days, she was hitched to the wagon, or the plow, depending on the season. She still loved the saddle, when she and George would take off on their own. Her easy, gliding walk carried them once again along the roads to town, church, and to call on neighbors.

One year, Fly raised a colt. She taught him everything she knew.

George married and had a family of his own. In Posey County, the log cabin days were ending. George's family was building a new house. Horses hauled wagonloads of crops away from the farm to sell, and brought in wagonloads of lumber from the sawmills, for the new buildings. There were also barrels of nails, and cast iron hardware.

Factories were making things for peacetime now, not war. There were fancy hinges with curly designs pressed into the metal, and hinge pins with pointy ends. There were glass windows, with sliding frames, and loads of bricks for the foundation. Horses pulled the big, flat shovel called a slip-scoop to dig the basement. The brick walls of the basement were built, and the wooden walls of the house were framed in. When it was finished, the house faced north,with two tall windows on either side of the front door. Siding boards covered the house, and it looked solid and whole. Inside, between the two big front rooms, there was a little entry room with stairs leading to the second floor. At the top of the stairs, a window looked out over the front yard, across Stewartsville Road, and down into the wooded valleys that led to the river bottoms. The front rooms were flooded with light from tall windows that reached from the floor almost to the ceiling.

Fly was a part of the house building. She helped grow the crops, haul them, and bring in the building materials. When it was time to plaster the walls, there was something else that she contributed.

Her fuzzy winter coat was brushed out, and all the loose horse hair was mixed into the plaster for the new house. This is how the plaster makers added strength to the mixture, so that it would not crack as it dried.

Hundreds of strips of wooden lath were nailed on the frame of two-by-fours inside the new house, and the men spread the wet plaster evenly over the wall. They would mix one batch at a time, so that it wouldn't set up and get hard before they finished. When the plaster was ready, wallpaper with pictures of flower bouquets was put up in the rooms. Curtains hung from the windows, and there were flowers planted in the yard.

Indiana was no longer the frontier. Now railroads ran across the land, connecting all sorts of places, the West was opened up, new states and territories were lined up to join the United States. The old canals were unused, and became backwaters, or were drained.

The Civil War was a turning point for America. In the remaining years of the 19th century, there were many exciting things that happened. But the veterans of the War between the North and the South knew that they had, indeed, "seen the elephant".

Veterans of the War formed groups to help take care of families that had lost their men. The G.A.R. was the group that George joined. The initials stood for the "Grand Army of the Republic". As well as making sure that widows and orphans were taken care of, the G.A.R. paid for monuments and reunions so that the veterans' sacrifices would not be forgotten.

Old Fly was taken to Civil War Reunions at Boonville, Indiana and to one at Albion, Illinois. She was taken to the local church at Bethsaida several times on Decoration Day, which is in May, when the peonies are in bloom, and people remember their loved ones who have died.

One time she went with George to nearby Cynthiana. Traveling reminded her of the war, when they had gone so far, and seen so many places.

These celebrations were special times for not only the veterans, but also the whole town. Families packed picnic lunches of cold fried chicken, biscuits, pies, and pickles and came to town in their wagons and buggies. Stores hung out flags and sold lemonade. Little boys ran around and

tried to see everything all at once. Mayors and preachers made speeches. The veterans wore their old uniforms, with the buttons polished. Once everyone was lined up for the parade, the band started to play, and the crowd along the street cheered.

Fly loved it.

When she heard the drums and trumpets, memories came rushing back. The wartime spirit lit up inside of her. She pranced, ready for the parade, just like in the old days at training camp. Her head was held high, and her eyes were full of fire. She listened for the horns to sound their signal, ready to charge into whatever she and George had to face.

These celebrations were when the men would remind each other of the stories they had lived. At the end of the long day, evening would come, and they would turn back homeward again.

In the everyday life after the war, George told his stories many times, and Fly was always in them. Fly herself remembered the excitement, action, and feelings. Those times that they had known would always be a part of the horse and her rider.

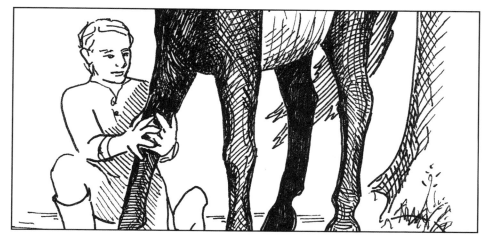

Chapter Fourteen
Old Fly

Age caught up with Fly, and people called her "Old Fly" now. Photographers came, to take her picture. She thought that they were mildly interesting, but nothing compared to what she had seen before. She'd raise her head and look at the camera, her white star still peeking out from behind her forelock. As she got older, it was harder to get up in the mornings, or even after resting in the middle of the day. Horses sleep standing up, but they still like to lie in the sun once in awhile, and the joints in Fly's knees were getting bad. Her front legs swelled with arthritis, and she needed extra care. George rubbed liniment on her knees to soothe the pain. He made sure that her hooves stayed trimmed, so that she could stand as comfortably as possible. Fly enjoyed the extra care, and it gave her time with George.

George rigged up a sling that fit under Fly's belly so that she could stand without putting weight on her legs. Her weight was held by the sling, and her feet still stood on the ground. In the summer, she would rest in her sling as it hung from a limb of one of the big maple trees in front of the house. Yes, George had always come up with interesting things for them to do together.

Fly spent her days enjoying the outdoors. Summer breezes waved their way across the hilltop fields, and lifted the forelock from her white star. Raising her nose to the wind, she sniffed the smell of the Black River flowing past the river bottom fields to the west of her home. She remembered how she would run through those fields, when she first came to this farm. How she would fly like the wind, up that road in front of the house, and away. With George on her back, she had flown so far. It was good to rest. She let the breezes come to her now.

She knew that she belonged to George, and that he would take care of her, as long as he could.

Towards the end, she would only eat sugar from George's hand. He bought her a barrel full of sugar, and fed her as much as she wanted.

In February of 1893, after the turning of the year, two months before she would be 39 years old, Fly took one last breath of the cold air, and she left behind her rider. She went ahead of him, after she had stayed as long as she could.

February is hard in Indiana. It is a time when winter won't let go. Spring is whispering in the trees, and buds may be swelling, but there is no comfort in the cold.

George's friend was gone. For the first time since he was just a boy, Fly was not there to brush and care for. Fly was not there to care for him. George was 52 years old. He had known Fly since he was 14.

At one corner of the farm, there stood a church called Bethesaida. Beside the church, a cemetery had headstones that told the names and dates of people's lives. Fly was buried on Bethesaida Hill, and the G.A.R. put a marker on her grave.

Bridgette Z. Savage

A life ends when the muscle and bone of a body give out. Fly and George had seen so many lives end early on the battlefields of the South. The old horse had out-lived all the hardships and adventures that the first part of her life held. Fly had lived a good life, far longer than most other horses. Her life had finally ended.

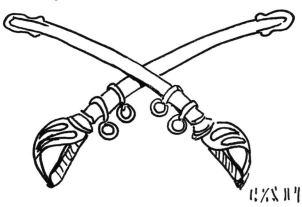

But when does a friendship end? A friendship is woven of memories, and George still had so many memories of Fly. Everyone for miles around had seen Fly, either because they knew the Barretts, or because they had seen Old Fly in the parades and Civil War Reunions. Old Fly was a veteran that everyone recognized. She was not an easy horse to forget. For George, she was a friend who would never be forgotten.

George and Fly were not the only horse and rider that had a special bond during the Civil War. Union General Sheridan had a big black charger named Rienzi, that led the troops to victory in the Shenandoah Valley. Rienzi was amazingly strong. When the men saw Sheridan ride into battle on the big horse, they forgot that they were tired, and fought with strength that they didn't know they had. After Rienzi died of old age in Chicago in 1878, General Sheridan donated his remains to a museum in New York. This way, his strength, and the bravery that Rienzi inspired in the soldiers would not be forgotten.

Traveller, Confederate General Lee's favorite horse, was a big gray. He carried his rider in victory and defeat, and followed him into life after the war. Lee became the president of Washington College, in Virginia. Eventually, the college changed its name to "Washington and Lee", in honor of the Southern General who was respected by both North and South. Traveller outlived Lee, and marched with his head held low, following the hearse in General Lee's funeral procession. After Traveller died, in 1875, his bones were housed at Washington and Lee College.

Union General Meade had a favorite horse called Baldy. That horse survived two wounds at Bull Run. He healed up in time to be in five more major battles. Then at Antietam, a huge hole was torn in his neck by artillery fire. The big horse fell to the ground and Baldy was left for dead on the battlefield. The next day, everyone was surprised to find him up and grazing. He was nursed back to health and carried the General in many more battles. At Gettysburg, a bullet went between his ribs and into his body. Still, he got well again. General Meade died in 1872 and, like Traveller, Baldy followed his master's funeral to the cemetery. When Baldy finally did die, his head and two front hooves were kept and preserved in Philadelphia.

Little Sorrel was the special horse of Confederate General "Stonewall" Jackson. First he was a Union Army horse, but was on board a train that was captured by the Rebels. General Jackson picked out two of the captured horses, and Little Sorrel ended up being his favorite. General Jackson was very tall, and this made Little Sorrel seem even smaller than he was. Little Sorrel certainly did not look like a superhorse, but looks don't always tell the whole story.

Not only was this little horse tough, he was brave and smart. Strength made up for size, and Little Sorrel carried the General until the day that Stonewall Jackson died on the battlefield. Throughout the war, and long after, Little Sorrel was known and loved by many people in the South. He lived more than twenty years after the war was over, and was shown in many fairs and parades. Finally, he got so weak that he had to be raised up in a sling each day. After Little Sorrell died, his remains were mounted and placed in the Virginia Military Institute Museum, alongside a display of the coat that General Jackson was wearing the day he died.

Fly had outlived all these other famous horses. The other horses had been kept in luxury by the generals that owned them, but Fly had just kept on working on the farm all those years. There is no way to explain why Fly lived so long, except that she liked being at home, with George.

It was a while before the decision was made that Fly should be remembered by more than a stone. With the help of a doctor, her bones were gathered and fitted together on an iron framework. Once again, Old Fly stood where she could be seen. George still wanted to take care of her, to put her someplace safe, and so the museum at the Working Men's Institute in New Harmony, Indiana became the new home for Old Fly. George could come and visit her any time of the day or night, if he wanted. And he did. He would often stand and look at his old friend's earthly remains. Thoughts of the future and memories of the past would mingle, and sometimes tears would slide down his cheeks.

Then there was a time when George came no more. He had followed Fly at last, leaving their story for us to know. George passed on to forever in 1930. The family donated Old Fly to the Working Men's Institute, so that it would always be her home.

There are many stories of the American Civil War. Many things were changed by that war, and will never be the same again. Some things were swept away, and lives that could have been good were ended. Beautiful places were turned to ugliness and sorrow. Even now, if we visit those places, the sadness hangs over them.

But even after the destruction of war, life went on.

George and Fly were lucky to have many years together after the war. Their story didn't end with the surrender of the South. The twenty-nine years they shared after the army were full of life. George had taken care of the little filly as long as he could, and done all that he could to make sure that she'd always be remembered and cared for.

Old Fly was a hard one to forget.

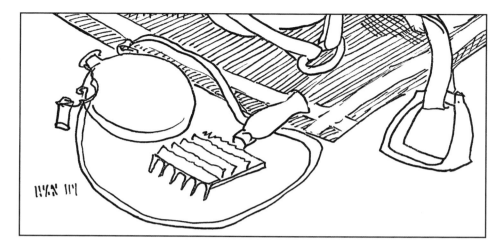

Epilogue

When I saw the display of Old Fly, with the McClellan saddle at her feet, I knew that there was more to the story of Old Fly and George M. Barrett than the battles they fought or the adventures they had. The photos of the horse and the man that were on top of the display case were both full of character. George and Fly were real, and they lived right there, near the very town I was visiting that day.

In the archives of the museum is a folder of photos, newspaper clippings and magazine articles about Old Fly.

The names and dates from those papers led me to books, and other stories. I read old newspapers from Posey County to see what life was like back then. The more I read and saw, the more real Fly and George became.

Their tale is filled with action and excitement. The best part, though, is the friendship that they shared.

The war adventures were told again and again in Fly's lifetime. After she was gone, George repeated the stories and kept her memory alive. Some hair from her tail was kept carefully wrapped, as a keepsake, and passed down through the family. Sometimes a school child would show up at George's grandson's house, and ask to borrow the hair for show-and-tell at school. And so Fly's life and times were known by whole classrooms full of students.

Two of George's daughters lived at the old farmhouse for many years, and kept a framed photo of Fly on an easel in the parlor. People who came to visit were told about the old horse. Those who heard about Fly remembered her, and told other people. Fly was talked about at Civil War reunions, family gatherings, homecoming dinners, in school history reports, in newspaper columns, and even in a magazine article. Grandparents sitting on front porches in the evenings told their grandchildren what they knew of her adventures.

The more we know about a person, or time, or place, the more we understand how it fits together with other things that we know. Stories are like puzzle pieces that make a larger picture when they are all put together. Although the Civil War was a long time ago, and Indiana has changed a lot since then, we can imagine what it was like for George and his friend to travel so far, and see so much.

Each of our lives touches another's. George and Fly's stories were locked together from the first moment they saw each other. Their story, and their lives, touched mine the moment I picked up the papers on the museum exhibit case in New Harmony.

A good story takes hold of something inside each person and makes it grow. Some are so good that they have to be shared.

And so, I put their story into this book in your hands. It is worth holding on to. And sharing.

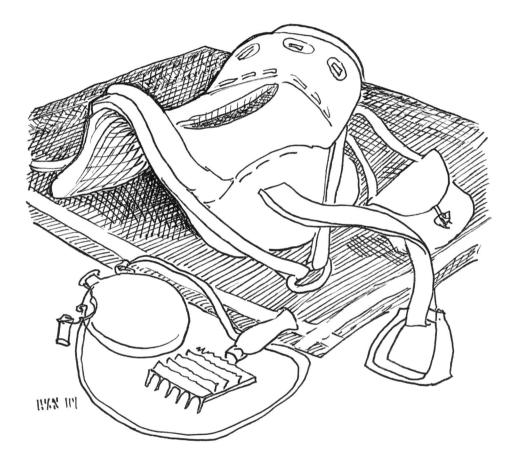

Acknowledgements

To my husband, a patient soul, willing traveling companion, and problem-solver. To my family, and their avid curiosities. To my mother, Cozette Evangeline Zahnle, for teaching me to stay with things, and to simply keep going onward.

With Appreciation to:

Mrs. Patricia Johnson, wife of Robert Johnson, who was a grandson of George M. Barrett. Without Mr. and Mrs. Johnson having kept the story alive, this book would not be possible. Sherry Graves and Frank Smith, of the Working Men's Institute in New Harmony, Indiana who were both very helpful on my visits to research Fly. My many friends and colleagues who took the time to read and make suggestions on the text and illustrations. Marianne and Larry Hughes, for their love of history and hard work. David Buchanan, Pam Chandler, and Donna Schmink, of the Col. Eli Lilly Civil War Museum in Indianapolis, Indiana for their encouragement and help with saddle blankets.

How Fly was Written

It is important to understand that my book, *Fly like The Wind*, is based on the oral history passed down and spread by the Barrett family and community members in and around Posey County. The skeleton of the book is the four-page account of the adventures of George W. Barrett and Fly which was donated to the Working Men's Institute, along with Fly's remains, by George's son, Carl, and his wife, Hortense, in July of 1930.

To bring the story to life, I read personal accounts of the Civil War in the Trans-Mississippi Campaign, looked at photos and battle field sketches that were made during the time Fly and George were enlisted, and read accounts of the battles and skirmishes in which the two took part.

Old Fly
1855-1893
Civil War Veteran
Company B, 1st Cavalry
28th Regiment Indiana Volunteers

Photo courtesy of Working Men's Institute
New Harmony, Indiana

George M. Barrett
1841-1929
Civil War Veteran
Company B, 1st Cavalry
28th Regiment Indiana Volunteers

Photo courtesy of Working Men's Institute
New Harmony, Indiana

© 2005 Buckbeech Studios

About the Author

Bridgette Z. Savage is a long-time resident of the beautiful hills of Southern Indiana. Growing up in a family that loves history gave her a life-long affection for small museums, old libraries, and roadside markers.

As an artist, author, and educator, she has a keen awareness of the way that stories can shape the way we see the world, and how we see ourselves.

After majoring in Fine Arts at Indiana University, she earned a teaching certification in Art Education, an endorsement in Gifted and Talented Education, and Master's degree in Counseling, with an Indiana Public Schools Counseling license.